Raffi Songs to Read™

EVERYTHING GROWS

Photo-illustrated by Bruce McMillan

Crown Publishers, Inc., New York

To Mother Earth for all she gives to help us grow.

Raffi

To everyone who celebrates life and living things.

Bruce McMillan especially thanks his playful young friends who appear in this book. The photographs were taken using a Nikon FE2 with Nikkor 35, 55 Micro, 105, or 200mm lenses, on Kodachrome 64 transparency film. The lighting is daylight accented with reflectors and/or fill flash.

Design by Bruce McMillan

Manufactured in the United States of America

Library of Congress Cataloging-in-Publication Data

Raffi. Everything Grows. Photographic illustrations and an original song show many different living things and their growth.
[1. Children's songs—Growth] [2. Fiction.]   I. Bruce McMillan, ill.   II. Title.
PZ8.3.R124Co   1989   [E]—dc19   88-37162
ISBN 0-517-57275-3 GLB/0-517-57387-3 Trade

10 9 8 7 6 5 4 3 2 1

First Edition

Everything grows and grows.

Babies do,

animals too.
Everything grows.

Everything grows and grows.
Sisters do,

brothers too.
Everything grows.

A blade of grass,

fingers and toes,

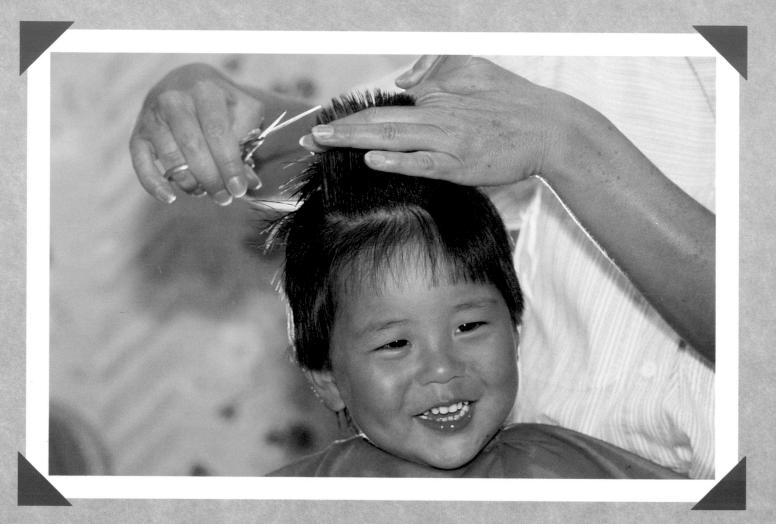

hair on my head,

a red, red rose.
Everything grows, anyone knows,
that's how it goes.

Everything grows and grows.
Babies do,

animals too.
Everything grows.

Everything grows and grows.

Sisters do, brothers too.
Everything grows.

Food on the farm,

fish in the sea,

birds in the air,

leaves on the tree.

Everything grows, anyone knows,

that's how it goes.

That's how it goes, under the sun.

That's how it goes, under the rain.
Everything grows, anyone knows,
that's how it goes.

Yes, everything grows and grows.
Babies do,

animals too.
Everything grows.

Everything grows and grows.

Sisters do, brothers too.
Everything grows.

Mamas do,

papas too.

Everything grows.

EVERYTHING GROWS

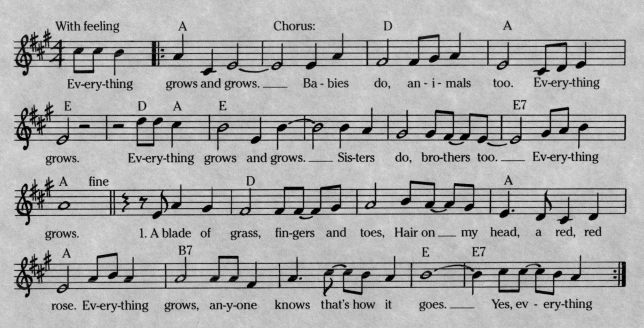

With feeling

Ev-ery-thing grows and grows. ___ Ba - bies do, an - i - mals too. Ev-ery-thing

grows. Ev-ery-thing grows and grows. ___ Sis-ters do, bro-thers too. ___ Ev-ery-thing

grows. 1. A blade of grass, fin-gers and toes, Hair on ___ my head, a red, red

rose. Ev-ery-thing grows, an-y-one knows that's how it goes. ___ Yes, ev - ery-thing

2 Food on the farm, fish in the sea,
Birds in the air, leaves on the tree.
Everything grows, anyone knows,
That's how it grows.

3 That's how it goes, under the sun.
That's how it goes, under the rain.
Everything grows, anyone knows.
That's how it goes.